I've Got This!

by Melisa Torres

Illustrated by Daniel Ramos

For my mom. Thank you for signing me up for
that first gymnastics class.

Melisa

Chapter 1

Round-Off Back Handspring on Floor

"She has only done a tumbling class," my mom informs the woman standing behind the desk.

"Where did she take tumbling?" the woman asks.

I listen to my mom explain that I took tumbling classes in California and that she is trying to find something for me to do now that we are in Utah. They start talking about our move with phrases like "Silicon Valley to Silicon Slopes" and "work-life balance." I'm tired of all of these lame explanations and I just want to do something fun instead of packing and unpacking.

I walk over and look through the double glass doors to the training area. There is an older girl, maybe a teenager, swinging around and around on the bars with her hands. She starts in a handstand, circles around, and ends in a handstand on that skinny little bar. All of a sudden she lets go of the bar and I suck in my breath as my stomach drops. Then she flips in the air and lands on her feet. I thought she messed up and was going to fall to her head, but she landed on her feet like a cat! That was totally awesome! My heart pounds in my ears just watching her. What must it feel like to *be* her? To flip from way up high like that?

I take a quick glance around to see who else saw what I just saw. I don't understand, no one in the entire training area noticed the super human trick she just did. Now she is quietly walking over mats to a bar sitting low on the ground. Another girl starts swinging on the bar as soon as the super human one flipped off. Why isn't anyone saying anything to her? Why aren't they telling her she is awesome? I feel my stomach clench a little. Do they think what she just did is *normal*?

I scan the rest of the gym and take a deep breath to calm myself down. I recognize most of the equipment from watching gymnastics on TV. When my heart stops pounding in my ears I can hear the woman ask my mom what skills I have and my mom saying she doesn't remember the names of the skills I learned at my tumbling studio.

"Trista," my mom calls to me.

I tear my eyes away from the action behind the glass doors and walk back to where they are talking.

"Hi, Trista. My name is Katie," the woman says directly to me. "What skills do you have?"

"I can do a round-off, two back handsprings, and an aerial," I answer proudly.

"Have you ever done the other events?" she asks.

"What are the other events?" I ask.

"Vault, uneven parallel bars, and balance beam," she answers.

"No," I say shaking my head, "I've only done tumbling on mats."

"Hmm, that's tricky." Katie says looking at my mom. "I don't recommend Level 1 because she is going to be so far ahead on floor," she says.

Then she turns to me, "With your tumbling experience you will probably catch up on the other events quickly. How old are you?" she asks me, tapping her pencil on her desk.

"Eight," I say "and I learn fast." I am getting more and more excited about the idea of swinging on those bars just like that girl was doing.

"Oh, yeah? Are you pretty strong too?" *Strong? I never thought about it.*

"Yes," I hear myself say. I will say anything to get myself in a class doing the cool flipping-off-the-bar stuff.

"Well, let's put you in Level 2 and see how it goes. You may even be able to move up to the Level 3 group quickly." *Sweet, I will move up to Level 3 before she knows it.*

"What do the levels mean?" my mom asks. *Good question,* I think as I focus on what Katie is going to say.

"The levels go from 1 to 10, not counting the pre-school ages. Pre-school kids have their own progression of levels. After Level 10 it goes to elite. Elite is what you see on TV. Unless you are watching college girls, they are Level 10."

"What level is she?" I ask, pointing to the girl who was doing those handstands on the bar into the flip. The girl is now standing with her hands in a tray of white dust talking to a teammate.

"Kayla? She's Level 8." Katie answers.

"That's it? She looks like the girls on TV to me," I exclaim and Katie laughs.

"She'll be pleased you said that. But gymnastics is a hard sport and there are a lot of skills and levels. Most people can't tell the difference between Level 8 and Level 10, but there is one," Katie explains.

"So what's the difference for Trista at Level 2 versus Level 3?" my mom asks.

"At PBGA, we let our girls start competing at Level 3. They have set routines they practice for competition. Level 2 is a more relaxed class, a good place for her to start. It would be a chance for Trista to catch up on the other events."

"What's PBGA?" I ask.

"Oh sorry, PBGA stands for Perfect Balance Gymnastics Academy and I am the owner," Katie smiles at me.

"And what if she gets to Level 3 but we don't want her to compete?" my mom continues.

"Mom! I want to compete!" I'm not sure how I know this already, but I do.

My mom looks down at me, "Well, how do you know? You might not. We need to get all the information."

I shrug because I don't have an answer, but I know. I just *know*! I want to be just like Kayla!

Katie smiles a knowing smile, like she is aware I have caught the gymnastics bug, "At Level 3 you can choose to start competing," Katie explains, "but you don't have to. We have about 15 girls in the Level 3 class, but only four have decided to compete this fall." My mom nods, listening closely. "In Levels 3, 4, and 5 all the kids across the nation have the same set routine. By Level 6, gymnasts get to do their own original routine. That's called Optionals; the practice hours really increase at that point. But you don't have to worry about that yet." *Oh yes we do! I am going to be a Level 10!*

"You can go up to the parent viewing area and take a look around, watch the practices that are going on," Katie offers.

"Okay, we'll do that," my mom agrees. "Thank you for explaining everything to us." Then she turns to me. "Do you want to go check it out?"

She doesn't need an answer because I am already pulling on her hand and heading to the stairs.

Chapter 2

Double Back on Floor

Once we are up in the viewing area I run to the windows and look at the gym below. I see Kayla walking away from the bar area and taking things off her hands. Since she is not doing anything interesting, I take in the rest of the gym. There is the floor to the far right with a big foam pit behind it at the right back corner. To the back there is a long strip of blue carpet running the length of the back wall and ending with a spring board and a big leather table. I think that is the vault. Then there are beams in the middle of the gym along with some equipment that I have seen on TV for boys, like the rings and a really high metal bar. The girl bars are situated to the far left and at the front of the gym there is a long red tumbling strip that runs the entire length of the gym.

I take more notice of the actual kids in the gym. There are kids everywhere! How do they not run into each other? Some are really little too. Coaches are yelling corrections or helping the kids with their tricks. Then I see Kayla and her team walking over to the floor area.

"This is quite an operation, huh Trista?" my mom comments. "Have you seen enough? Are you ready to go?"

"I want to see what those girls do next," I say pointing to what must be the Level 8 group.

"Okay, couple more minutes and then we have to go."

As we watch the Level 8's get started on floor, our jaws drop. They tumble so cleanly and perfectly. We know tumbling. I have been doing tumbling. But nothing like this. These girls make a round-off back handspring back tuck look so easy. And they get so high.

After a few minutes their tricks get harder and harder. They are now straightening out their back flip to a layout and some of the girls start twisting in the air during their layout. I don't even know what that is called, but I know I want to do it.

Then a couple of the girls start tumbling into the foam pit area. They do a round-off back handspring on the floor and flip into the pit. They are doing really high back tucks into the pit and I wonder why because their back tucks looked perfect on floor. Then the coach walks over and stands on the edge of the floor and the pit. He yells some things to Kayla, who is standing at the other end of the floor ready to go. Kayla nods and starts her pass. She does her round-off back handspring and instead of doing one flip into the pit she does two flips, *rotates two times,* before she lands in the fluffy pit.

"Did you see that?" I ask my mom with so much excitement I don't even recognize my own voice.

"Yes," she confirms, "and I don't *ever* want to see you doing that."

Too late. It's going to happen.

"You should have seen these girls; they were so cool!" I say excitedly to my dad as we sit down to dinner.

"So you think this is something you want to do?" he asks.

"No, I *know* this is something I want to do!" I respond.

"How do you know?" my older sister asks, with her favorite condescending voice.

"I know I like tumbling and what they were doing looks even better," I say as I cross my arms and give her my dirtiest look.

"Yeah, but you haven't even tried the other events yet. What if you're *horrible* at them?" she counters, dragging out the word horrible.

"Madison, there is no need for that," my mom cuts in.

"Well, I just think she is getting a little carried away," my know-it-all-turd-bucket sister says.

"She's just excited," my mom defends. "It's great to be excited about something."

It *is* great to be excited about something. I have my first gymnastics practice on Wedesday and I am going to prove my sister wrong. I am going to be great at bars and beam and vault! This will be so easy.

Chapter 3

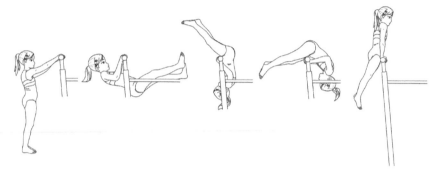

Pullover on Bars

This is not so easy. I hate it when my sister is right.
Bars are harder than they look. We warmed up and
went to bars first. We are working on a set of four low
bars, called the quad bars, and there are two of us
to a bar trying to do what is called a pull over. I am
supposed to pull my chin up to the bar and then my
feet up and over my head until I circle around and find

myself up in a support position on the bar. But all I seem to do is kick my feet up and they flop down again. So I decide to just jump up on the bar and swing around on my waist.

"Trista, what skill are you working on over there?" My coach, Melony, calls out. *I dunno, just having a little fun.*

"I got up here, so I just started swinging," I reply.

"Did you get up there doing a pull over?" she asks.

"Yeah! I did!" I fib.

"Great, let's see it." Uh-oh. I hadn't thought about that when I decided to fib a little. I get down and put my hands on the bar and I am determined to make this pull over to save myself the embarrassment of being caught in a lie. I kick my feet up and my body flops them back down. Melony comes over to me. "Try again," she instructs. "Only this time instead of throwing your head back, look at the bar." I try again exactly how she says. I kick my feet up and keep my eyes on the bar, my feet go much farther up this time, I feel her hand on the small of my back as she pushes me up and over. "That was much better. Keep doing it like that and you'll have it in no time." I smile sheepishly, impressed at how nice she is about my stupid liar-pants big mouth.

"Carmen, you can move onto casts and back hip circles," my coach says to the girl sharing the bar with me. "Trista, try a couple more pull overs then you can go on to casts too, Carmen can show you."

I look over at Carmen. She has big brown eyes and a ton of dark brown hair along with beautiful olive skin. She is wearing an adorable shimmering black leotard with orange and yellow butterflies on it. It makes me feel lame in my simple blue and red leotard. My mom wouldn't buy me a new leotard in case I don't stick with it.

"This is a cast," Carmen says as she supports herself on the bar with straight arms and swings her legs back and forth until the momentum brings her hips off the bar.

"Okay," I say as I jump up to the bar. I do one or two, but my hips don't come off the bars like hers did,

17

so I lose interest and jump down and start swinging

below the bar. Carmen is still working on the casts

and I want her attention, "How long have you been in

gymnastics?" I ask.

"A year," she answers.

"And you have been in this class all along?" I ask

She stops doing her casts long enough to look

at me like I am asking a silly question, "No. I started in

Level 1. This is my first day in Level 2."

"Oh." I say, and I remember that I started in Level

2 because of my tumbling experience.

"How old are you?" I ask.

"Eight," she says between casts. This girl never

stops for a break.

"Me too!" I say with glee. Another girl my age; this

is great news. I look at the rest of the girls in our class

and they look really young, five or six maybe. Carmen

and I are definitely the oldest girls in this class.

"Good job Carmen, you can move on to back

hip circles," Melony calls out. "Trista, let me see a cast,"

she orders. I jump up to the bar again and try casting,

but I know I am not doing it right. Melony comes over to me again and spots me so they look more like Carmen's casts.

Then we work back hip circles and swing downs, all of which I cannot do. Of course, I will not share this information with my sister.

We finish up bars and go over to the beams. "When are we going to floor?" I ask, knowing this is where I am going to shine. I know what I'm doing when it comes to tumbling. And the floor here is softer and springier than the tumbling studio I went to in San Jose.

"After beam, when the Level 3's are done with the floor area," she answers. I look over at the Level 3's and notice they are more my age. They are all working round-off back handsprings. They look like they are having so much fun and all of a sudden I am sad I am with a bunch of 5-year-olds. After all, I am eight. What do I need to do to get out of this class?

Chapter 4

Cross Handstand on Beam

"Grab a beam," Melony says to me, pointing to one of the two beams sitting on the ground.

"We aren't going to a regular beam?" I ask, gesturing to the tall beams that I have seen on TV.

She smiles. "We will in a bit Trista, but for now we are going to warm up on the low beams and work some basic skills before we spend time on the high beams." She turns to Carmen and says, "Carmen and Emma, you two can do these drills on the medium beam."

I am bummed at this boring turn of events as I take a 6 inch step up onto a low beam. But after about five minutes I am glad Melony was smart enough to have us on the low beams, because I have a hard time staying on the little beam on the ground. Every few seconds I am stepping off of it. She has us doing all kinds of things on that skinny beam. Skipping, hopping, jumping, running, bear-walking, and even handstands. It is crazy. The beam is much more narrow than it looks.

"How wide is the beam?" I ask.

"Four inches wide," Melony says, "not much room for error, so you have to pay attention." *No kidding, I figured that out on my own.*

"Okay girls, let's do some forward and backward walks on the high beam." The other girls in my class run over and jump up on the high beams and start walking. I stay put on my puny little safe-on-the-ground beam.

"Trista, aren't you coming?" Melony asks. I shake my head slowly. "I thought you were excited to get up on the high beam," she says confused.

"That was before I knew how hard it is. I couldn't stay on this beam without stepping off, which would be falling off up there," I say, pointing to the big beams.

"It's not as bad as it looks. How about I hold your hand?" Melony suggests.

How about I stick to tumbling. Then I see Kayla out of the corner of my eye flipping off the vault table and I know I want to do all the events, not just floor. So I nod and let my coach lead me over to the big beam. I climb up slowly and wobble as I stand up. It is scary and exhilarating up here, the gym looks so different. She lifts up her hand and I take it. I take a tiny step forward and smile at her.

"Watch the beam, not me. You want to make sure you are walking straight." *Good point, watch the beam, watch the beam . . . I am doing it!* And it feels great. I let go of her hand and keep going. This isn't so bad.

"Good Trista, now walk backwards," she says. I stop walking; *is she serious? Walk backwards?*

"But you just said to watch the beam, how do I do that walking backwards?" I ask and I look over to my teammates and they are motoring across the beams on their tippy toes. Show offs.

Melony chuckles and says, "When you walk backwards you watch the end of the beam in front of you, this keeps you moving straight." I nod at this logic, but don't move. "Put one foot behind you and when your toes feel the beam and you know it's behind you, transfer your weight to that foot." She explains.

I tentatively put one foot behind me and I feel the rough leather under my toes. I very slowly step back onto that foot. *I did it!* I am so impressed with myself, but Melony doesn't seem impressed because she doesn't say anything and I can feel her watching. "Again," she says. Okay, okay, another step. I take my other foot and put it behind me and feel for the beam. I feel it under my toes, so I step back.

"Keep it up until I get back, I'm going to help these girls over here with their form," Melony instructs, as she lets go of my hand. I hear her step over to the other beams and correct the girls on their bent knees. I'm not sure how you walk with straight knees, but that's not my concern now as I slowly inch along the beam backwards. This is agony; this isn't fun. How do girls do real tumbling up here? That thought distracts me and all of a sudden I feel myself wobble and fall off the beam. I land on my feet, which I guess is not that surprising since I was just standing in the first place.

I glance over to Melony, "How tall is beam? How high up was I?" I ask. "Because it felt really high."

"Okay girls, get a drink and head to floor" she says to everyone. *Yay! Floor!* She walks over to me. "The beam is four feet off the ground, four inches wide, 16 feet long. I love your curiosity," she tells me as we walk over and step up onto the floor. "Anything else you're curious about?"

As I step up onto the floor it is soft and bouncy. I lift up on my toes and do a little bounce. "Yeah," I say, "why is your floor bouncier than a regular floor?" I ask.

"It has springs."

"Seriously? Isn't that cheating?" I ask.

"No, it's not cheating because every gymnastics floor has springs. They are little 6 inch coils all over the floor. Under the carpet we are standing on is a foam mat, then ply wood, then the springs, and then a hard concrete floor," she explains.

"But why are there springs? So we can get higher?" I ask.

"Actually, it helps more with shock absorption and saving your joints; the higher tumbling is just a side benefit."

Shock absorption. Interesting, I never thought about joints before. But now that I do think about it, my wrists did hurt sometimes in my old tumbling class. I wonder what it will feel like here. And then I realize it's time to practice floor and I'm done chit-chatting. "Can I tumble now?"

She laughs, "You are a funny one. Get a drink and meet me back here."

Chapter 5

Aerial on Floor

We are on the bouncy floor but all we are working are round-offs and cartwheels.

"Melony, I know how to do a round-off back handspring," I say.

"Great news. Let me see your round-off first," she fires back at me. I do my round-off. "When you can do that with your legs together and your bum tucked under, then you can move onto round-off back handsprings." *What? I have to keep doing round-offs?*

"But I can do a round-off back handspring,"
I persist.

"I'm sure you can, but you're sloppy. Time to start cleaning things up. Do a clean round-off and you can move on." Sheesh, she is intense. My other gym just let us move on when we weren't scared. After goofing around for a bit I decide to try a clean round-off. I look up to smile at Melony and she's moved away. She missed it!

"You missed it!" I whine.

"Trista, how many girls do you see here?" She is waiting for an answer.

"Eight," I huff.

"Yes, eight. My job is to watch everyone. Your job is to do a skill over and over and eventually I will see it, okay?" she explains.

"Yeah, okay. But I did it." I just can't drop it.

"Good, keep doing it until I come back to you," she says as she walks over to the other girls. This place is serious. I stand stunned for a minute but then I decide to keep doing clean round-offs like she said because I want to move on to working round-off back handsprings. After about my third or fourth one, I hear, "Beautiful Trista, you may go on to round-off back handsprings." I look up and smile. She was watching and I didn't even know it. She doesn't have to tell me twice to move on. I back up on my little strip of space on the floor and run and do a round-off back handspring. They are so fun!

"Wow, Trista, those are really nice. It looks like you have enough power for two back handsprings. Can you do two?" Melony asks. I nod with a huge smile. "Well, let's see it."

I back up and do my pass with two back handsprings. "Great!" she exclaims. "You just need to clean them up a little and then I will teach you a back tuck."

"You can do that? In a Level 2 class?" I ask delighted.

"Sure, whenever you finish the assignment, I'll let you move on. I can teach all the levels, there's no reason you can't learn something during our floor rotation, too," she explains. "What other surprises do you have for me?" she asks.

I grin and start backing up, "An aerial," I say.

"How was your first day at gymnastics?" my dad asks as I am setting the table.

"It was awesome. I knocked my coach's socks off with my tumbling!" I exclaim.

"I bet you did; you can do some amazing stuff. What about the other events?" he questions.

"Oh, fine," I say as I set out the napkins next to the paper plates (we still haven't unpacked the kitchen all the way and my mom doesn't know what boxes the plates are in).

"Just fine? What happened?" my dad asks.

"Well," I hesitate because my sister is within earshot, but my dad is waiting for an answer. "It was hard."

"Haha! I told you!" the turd-bucket exclaims.

"Madi," my dad warns. Then he looks at me. "Of course it was hard. Everything is hard on the first day. But did you have fun?"

"Well, yeah. I got to walk on the really high beam and that was cool. I learned some stuff on bars. I can't do them yet, but swinging around was fun," I answer honestly.

"Then stick with it this summer and see what happens. It will probably get easier as you get used to it," he says. This makes me feel a little better to know I have the whole summer stretched out in front of me.

But there is one other thing that is bothering me and I frown as I think about it. "What else?" Dad says as he sees my frown.

"I'm older than the girls in my group. I don't like it. All the girls, except one, are like, five. I want to be with the Level 3 girls," I confess.

"Then you better work extra hard to catch up," he says as he turns on the news.

Chapter 6

Handstand Forward Roll on Floor

After dinner I wander outside in the warm summer evening to eat a Popsicle on the front porch. It is a quiet street and the mountains here are huge and interesting to look at. They are green at the base, gray rock in the middle, and the tippy-top is white with snow on the peaks. I guess our green 'mountains' back home were really just hills. As I am managing the mess of the end of a Popsicle I hear girls laughing and giggling. I look around and finally see them on the front grass two houses down.

"Your turn," I hear one of the girls yell.

"Okay," a little blond girl says as she scoots back to the edge of the grass. Then she runs and does a round-off back handspring.

"Your knees were bent; I give you an 8.5," the other girl says. This comment gives them away, they are gymnasts. I take a closer look and study them. I recognize the blond; she was the smallest one in that Level 3 group. And the other girl looked familiar too.

I get up and run inside. "Mom! Mom!" I yell.

"What is it?" My mom appears at the top of the stairs.

"There are girls next door, and I think they're gymnasts. Can I go meet them?" I rush the words out so fast it takes her a minute to process what I said.

"Sure, let me go with you," she says as she turns away from me.

"Where are you going? They might go back inside!" I shriek.

"Just getting my shoes, calm down."

Finally, she comes to the front door and we walk past our neighbor's house to the house where I saw the girls playing. We can hear the girls still laughing and scoring each other.

"What do I say?" I whisper to my mom.

"Hello," she says simply.

"Hello," my mom says as we walk up, "we just moved into that house right there," my mom says, pointing to our house. "Which one of you girls lives here?" she asks.

"I do," the blond says. She is a pretty girl. Her eyes are a really bright blue and she has a pert little nose, the kind I have always wanted.

"Hello neighbor, my name is Andrea, and this is my daughter, Trista. What's your name?" My mom is so smart, how does she always know just what to say?

"I'm Savannah," the blond girl says. She is looking at me with curiosity, but I don't know what to say to her.

"Nice to meet you Savannah," my mom continues. "And your friend is?" she asks.

"This is Marissa," Savannah answers.

"Nice to meet you Marissa," my mom says. Then she turns back to Savannah, "Is your Mom or Dad home?" she asks.

"My mom is," Savannah offers.

"May I meet her?" my mom asks.

"Sure," Savannah says and bounds off. This leaves us alone with Marissa and it is silent for a second. Marissa is a pretty girl, too, not cute like Savannah, but more exotic looking. I can tell she is part Asian from her round face, almond eyes, and dark hair, but there is something else about her that makes her really unique. As I try to place what it is, she pulls her black hair out of its ponytail and begins to retie it. I have never seen so much glossy, slippery hair. I wish my hair was like Marissa's or Savannah's. Mine is a boring straight brown. At least my eyes are an interesting hazel with olive and yellow, my grandma always tells me they look like cat eyes.

"Marissa," my mom starts, "we saw you guys doing some great tricks over here. Do you do gymnastics?" she asks.

"Yes," Marissa answers.

"Where do you take lessons?" my mom continues with ease.

"At Perfect Balance Gymnastics Academy," she answers.

"That's where Trista started just today," my mom says.

"Really?" Marissa turns to me, those dark eyes so serious. "What class are you in?"

"Level 2," I mumble. I'm a little embarrassed that I'm only Level 2 because I know I saw her in the Level 3 class and she looks my age, maybe even younger.

"I just barely moved up from that class. I finally got my pullover. It took me forever," she says, making me feel better.

"Those are hard, I was working on them today," I say. I feel very cool that I know what a pullover even is.

"Hello," a woman says to us as she is coming out of the house with Savannah. "I'm Debbie, Savannah's mom," she says extending her hand.

"I'm Andrea, your new neighbor," my mom says, "and this is my daughter, Trista."

"Nice to meet you, Trista," she says warmly. "So glad to have another girl in the neighborhood. It's all boys around here." At this Savannah makes a face and it makes me giggle.

"Where did you move from?" Debbie asks. Here we go again. I am so tired of talking about our move. My mom starts answering Debbie with the same responses I have already heard a million times. Dad got an offer to transfer to Snowcap Canyon for more money and the cost of living is lower in Utah than in California, so now mom can stay home with us, blah, blah, blah.

"What are you guys playing?" I ask the girls, hoping to drown out the adults and their boring conversation about how hard it must be to uproot an entire family.

"A gymnastics game, want to play?" Marissa asks.

"Sure, how do you play?" I ask.

"You do a skill and we judge it. You can just do a cartwheel or whatever," she explains.

"Okay," I say, knowing I can impress them with more than a cartwheel. I back up to get a good run and I start to go and Savannah yells for me to stop. "What?" I ask, confused.

"You have to salute the judge," she says raising her hand to me.

"What is that?"

Savannah smiles. "In a meet you salute the judge by raising your arm to tell her you're ready. Well, actually, she salutes first to tell you she is ready, and then you salute back," she quickly explains. "I am your judge," she says, raising up her arm.

I start giggling at her extra-serious expression and raise my arm back at her. Then I start my run and I throw an aerial.

"Whoa! Ten! Ten!" Savannah jumps up and down.

"I thought you said you were a Level 2? Why are you in Level 2 if you can do that?" Marissa asks.

"I did a tumbling class before, but I've never done the other events, so I have to catch up."

"Catch up fast, because it would be fun to have my neighbor on my team," Savannah says as she runs to the end of the grass. "My turn, who's judging?" she says as she raises her hand to me.

Savannah runs and does a round-off back handspring. Then looks at me expectantly. I'd forgotten I was supposed to judge her. "Um, 9?" I say.

"Whoo hoo," Savannah says and runs over to us and sticks out her tongue at Marissa.

"No way," Marissa says. "Your legs were bent and apart; that was an 8.0 at best. Why did you give her a 9?" Marissa asks me.

"I'm not sure. I don't really know how a judge decides," I confess.

"Okay, okay," Marissa laughs. "Start at a 10 and for every mistake - like bent knees, flexed feet, and legs apart - take off half a point."

"Is that really how it works?" I ask.

"It's way more complicated than that, but we're just playing," Savannah explains.

"I think you gave Savannah a 9 for cute points," Savannah's mom adds. I look at Savannah in her bright pink tank top and pink and lime swirl gymnastics shorts. She has little muscles I have never seen on a kid before. She *is* really cute. But I am embarrassed to admit it.

"She just looked cool doing her trick," I say.

"Our coach says not to call them tricks," Marissa adds.

"What are they then?" I ask.

"Skills. It's not magic, so it's not a trick. They are skills because we work hard to learn them," she explains.

This makes sense, but I am starting to get a little overwhelmed. There is so much to learn; so much terminology.

"Okay, Marissa, your turn," Savannah says. "I will be judge with Trista so she can learn how to do it," she says.

Marissa backs up and does a leap, a cartwheel, and a handstand forward roll. Savannah turns her blue eyes to me, "Her form was good, but her split leap wasn't very split. What do you think?"

"8.7?" I guess

"8.7!" Savannah yells out and then to me. "Your turn." I grin. This is fun.

Chapter 7

Split Leap on Beam

This is no fun; summer can get boring. My mom took us swimming this morning, but we are inside this afternoon just hanging out. I wander into my parent's bedroom where my mom is folding laundry. "Mom, do you want to play a game?" I ask, even though I know odds are slim.

"Not right now, I'm trying to finish laundry before the weekend," she predictably answers. "If you are bored I can think of plenty of things for you to do," she adds.

"I'm not bored," I lie as I hightail it out of there before she makes me dust something. I wander into my sister's room next out of sheer desperation. "Hey, Madison, do you want to play a game?"

"Not really," she says as she scrolls through a list of music on her phone. Her headphones are around her neck and she is slouched on her bed. I know she'll be sitting there for a while, doing nothing, which I don't get. Madison used to be so much more fun, now she is so secretive and lazy. My mom says it's a teenage thing.

I'm making my way back to my quiet room when the doorbell rings. I run to the door, "I'll get it!" I know it's probably the UPS guy, but I'm excited anyway. I open the door and standing there is Savannah. "Hey," I say with a smile.

"Hi," she says shyly. "I came to see if you wanted to come to Parents' Night Out tonight."

"What's Parents' Night Out?" I ask.

"It's at Perfect Balance on Friday nights. Parents can drop their kids off and we get to run around and play on the equipment in ways we are not allowed to in class. It's super-fun," she explains.

"Mom!" I yell up to my mom. My mom is already walking up behind me because she heard the doorbell.

"That sounds fun Savannah; thanks for thinking of Trista. Do you know what time it starts and how much it costs?" my mom asks.

"No," Savannah answers honestly.

"Well, is your Mom home? I can come over and ask."

"No, she's at work. My grandma is home though. She might know," Savannah adds.

I look closely at Savannah; she seems shy and nervous right now, which is weird because we had so much fun playing outside the other night.

"Do you know your mom's number so I can call her, or do you want to run back and ask your grandma?" my mom asks.

"I'll go ask my grandma," she says, and runs off our porch and is halfway to her house before I can blink.

I turn to my mom, "Can I go? Please, please, please?"

"Stop begging, and let's talk about it," she says. I immediately stop. My mom hates it when I beg, but I always do it anyway. I honestly don't know why; it has never gotten me what I want. "Since I don't know how much it costs or what time it starts, I cannot promise you anything," she says. "But we have nothing going on tonight so you can probably go. Let's see what Savannah comes back and tells us."

I pace outside waiting for Savannah to come back. Finally she skips back up to the door and tells us the details of Parents' Night Out and my mom agrees to let me go. My mom says she can drive us there if Savannah's mom or grandma can pick us up. We're all set; I can't wait!

Chapter 8

Fly Spring on Floor

"Bye girls, be safe," my mom says, as she leaves
us at Perfect Balance's Parents' Night Out. We put our
flip flops in a cubby and walk into the training area. I
look around and there are kids everywhere, doing all
sorts of crazy things on the gymnastics equipment. Big
kids, little kids, boys, girls, teenagers; some are doing
real gymnastics skills, some are just goofing around,
and some of the teenagers are talking in a circle. It's

loud in here, with blaring music and squealing kids. It's also freezing in the gym. I shiver and look at Savannah. "What do you want to do first?" I ask.

"The pit!" she yells and runs along the red tumble strip, over to floor, and across the floor. I run after her and we jump into the pit. It's full of fluffy foam squares. As we are struggling to get out I see Marissa run over and jump in. "Hey Marissa, are Alexis and Paige coming?" Savannah asks.

"I think Alexis might; Paige said she couldn't this weekend." Marissa answers.

We finally get ourselves out of the pit only to run and jump in again a few more times. Now I'm hot in here; I'm sweating from all this running, jumping, and climbing.

I feel like I have just discovered the greatest kids' adventure ever in this Parents' Night Out. I'm having so much fun with my two new friends, Savannah and Marissa.

"Let's go to trampoline," Marissa suggests and we walk across the floor to the front of the gym, along the red tumbling strip, over to the in-ground trampoline.

"Hey James," Marissa says to a man standing on the edge of the trampoline. I can tell he is a coach right away because he is standing on the edge of the trampoline watching a gymnast very carefully. He is wearing a backwards hat, athletic shorts, and a Nike T-shirt.

"Hey ladies." He greets us without taking his eyes off the gymnast on trampoline. I follow his gaze to look at her and just then she does a full twisting back flip. It's amazing and awesome and I will never tire of watching the athletes here.

"Good. End on that one. Grip up for bars," James says to the girl. Then he swings his hat around to the front and looks down at us. "You here to work your leaps on beam?" he asks, with a twinkle in his gray eyes.

"Yeah, right," Marissa fires back, "we're here to have fun."

James chuckles, and notices me. "Who's your friend?"

"That's Trista, she's new." Savannah answers.

"Hello, Trista," James says, turning to me. "I'm James, Savannah and Marissa's coach. What are you new to? Gymnastics, PBGA, or Snowcap Canyon?" he asks.

"All of it, sort of," I answer.

"All of it, sort of." he repeats. "What's the sort of? Hey, one at a time!" he interrupts our conversation to get two boys off the trampoline who are not following the rules of the gym. "You two are going to knock heads. You get off," he says to one boy. Then he says to the other, "when he's done, you can have a turn, and then these girls want a turn." After one of the boys jumps off the trampoline and the other one is safely jumping again, James turns to me, "What's the sort of?"

"Well, I did tumbling, but not gymnastics," I explain.

"Oh, yeah? Where'd you tumble?" he asks.

"In San Jose."

"You any good?" he asks.

"I guess" I say a little more shyly than I'm used to. Around regular people I would give a definite yes, but around all these gymnasts their idea of 'good' is so much different.

"How old are you?" he asks out of the blue.

"Eight," I say.

"Eight, going on 13 based on those one word answers," he says, and I'm not sure what he means but I don't think it's a compliment.

"She's good," Marissa pipes in. She and Savannah are standing right next to me as we wait for a turn on the trampoline.

"Well let's see then," James says. "But no trying anything you have never done before. No getting hurt. I don't want to deal with an injury tonight."

I smile. "Okay," I say and I skip over to the tumbling strip. I run and do a nice round-off back handspring.

"Not bad," he yells, "now do it with straight legs and pointed toes," he says. Determined to get a real compliment I go back and do it again and I actually think about my form. "Better. You have hope," James says and turns back to Savannah to tell her it is her turn on the trampoline. I'm not sure what to make of that so I go back to the red tumbling strip and run and do an aerial. I look around and no one says anything. So I go back over to Marissa and James.

"Did you see my aerial?" I ask James.

"Yes," he says without taking his eyes off Savannah on the trampoline. "Bring your chest up when you land and look at a spot on the wall. You'll land it better."

"Oh," I say defeated.

He looks down at me, "What class are you in?"

"Level 2," I say quietly.

"Well, keep coming to Parents' Night Out and Open Gym and you'll be Level 3 in no time, especially if I'm here to give you corrections."

"What's Open Gym?" I ask.

"Open Gym is held the two hours before PNO, from 4 to 6. It's a little more structured for our gymnasts to work on skills they have been struggling with. Open Gym has more coaches on staff and often there are private lessons going on. PNO is more of a crazy free for all where non-gymnasts and kids from other gyms can come and play on the equipment." James explains. "Anna, it's Marissa's turn, stop being a tramp hog," he says to Savannah.

I watch Savannah jump off and Marissa jump on to the trampoline. Marissa immediately starts doing back handsprings connected to fly-springs.

"What do I have to do to be a Level 3?" I ask.

"What can you do on the other events?" I pause because Savannah is standing right next to me and I'm embarrassed to admit my complete failure to do anything on the other events.

"Well, I just started this week . . . ," I stall.

He laughs, and nods. "Anna, go set up the mats for vault; let's teach your friend how to vault tonight."

"By myself?" she whines. "James, we're here to have fun."

"Then tell Katie not to make me work Parents' Night Out," he laughs. "Show Trista how to set it up.

53

Marissa, get off the trampoline and help your friends,"
he orders.

"Why does he call you Anna?" I ask Savannah
as I follow her to get the mats. I'm not sure where we
are going or what we are getting, but Savannah and
Marissa seem to know.

"He doesn't like long names," Savannah answers.
"He says it takes him too long to yell out corrections. So
he shortened Savannah to Anna. My mom hates it, but
I kind of like it."

"Do you have a shorter name?" I ask Marissa.

"Yeah, it took him a while. I was Riss, then Rissy.
Lately he has been using Li, which is my last name."

"Which one do you like the most?" I ask curious.

She laughs, "Marissa, I like Marissa the most." She
is silent for a minute and then says, "But Li is okay too. It
makes me feel like the athletic boys on the playground.
They all call each other by their last names."

The girls stop over by a stack of mats that are
sitting near floor exercise and start tugging at the top of
one. Savannah and I are pulling and Marissa is on the

other side pushing. As we get the mat off the stack and it plops to the ground, a teenager breaks from their talking circle and yells, "Who wants to do a back tuck stick contest?" A bunch of kids run forward.

"What is that?" I ask Marissa and Savannah.

Before they can answer me an older boy runs by us and says, "You guys in?"

"We're too little," Marissa answers. "We can't do them yet."

"We can't do what?" I ask.

"Let's just sit right here on the 8 incher and watch," Savannah says sitting on the mat we just dropped on the edge of the floor.

"Watch what?" I screech. My voice is getting higher as I get frustrated about not knowing what's going on. Marissa flops on the mat, lays down next to Savannah, and puts her chin in her hands. Savannah swivels around onto her tummy and also puts her chin in her hands.

"Have a seat, Trista, you'll see," Savannah says, looking up at me.

I sigh and join them on the mat. I watch as the older kids form themselves in a wide circle on the big spring floor. "Winner buys pizza," the boy who called for the contest says.

"We already have pizza, genius," one of the girls says.

"Well, think of something else then," he counters

"Winner gets a leotard from the Pro Shop," she says looking at James slyly.

"Nice try Liz," James says, walking over to the floor from the trampoline. "Winner gets bragging rights for the night. Now get going so the little kids can use the floor again."

Liz raises her arms up, lifts up on her toes, jumps up and flips backwards, landing easily on her feet. Holy cow! She just stood there and did a back flip. Immediately the next gymnast, Kayla, in the circle does the same thing. Then the next kid, and the next. I couldn't believe my eyes, it was so cool how they did that.

"What exactly are they doing?" I ask the girls.

"A standing back tuck sticking contest," Savannah answers.

"If you don't stick your back tuck you're out" Marissa explains. "If you stick it, then it keeps going until there is only one person left and they are the winner."

"What does sticking it mean?" I ask.

"Not moving your feet on the landing," Savannah says without taking her eyes off the contest.

Wow. Gymnastics is so cool.

Chapter 9

Standing Back Tuck on Floor

"You should have seen them all doing back flips so easily! Oh, and I learned the Level 3 vault and did back tucks in the pit. James says that if I keep going to PNO that I could be Level 3 in no time. So can you keep taking me? Puh-leese!" I beg.

"Whoa, slow down," my mom says. Savannah's mom brought me home from Parents' Night Out and I just walked in the door. It's late, and my parents are sitting on the couch cuddling. They were watching a movie, but paused it when I walked in.

"What's PNO?" my dad asks, chuckling.

"Parents' Night Out, duh, Dad. So, can I go again next week?"

"Trista, we don't have to decide this right now, why don't you wind down and go to bed and we can talk about it in the morning." He dismisses me.

Then my mom adds, "Why the rush to Level 3? Just enjoy the summer in Level 2."

"Because my friends are in Level 3, and all the other kids my age. If I want to compete this fall, I need to be Level 3," I explain.

"Hang on, who said anything about competing?" my mom asks.

"Kate, or Katie, the lady who greeted us, she said Level 3 competes," I remind her.

"She said some Level 3s compete if they want. I'm not sure that is what's right for you. It's a big commitment," she says.

"What!" I shriek, "Why would you put me in gymnastics and then not let me do it?" I demand.

"I am letting you do gymnastics, just not - ,"

"Okay, guys," my dad cuts us off, "can we talk about this tomorrow?" He can see we are getting heated up. Why is my mom being so stubborn? "Go on up to bed Trista," my dad orders, "We can talk tomorrow."

I stomp up the stairs and with a dramatic yell at each stair, I say, "This. Is. So. Not. Fair!" And I slam the door for flair.

A few minutes later my sister pokes her head in. "What's going on drama queen?" she asks.

"Shut up," I say as I get my pajamas on. She walks in a little further.

"Seriously, Trista, why are you acting like a teenager, what's going on?" She seems to be asking because she really cares, which is why the turd-bucket throws me off. I think sometimes she really does care.

"That is the second time someone has compared me to a teenager today," I say, plopping on the bed.

"Well? Is that a bad thing?" she says with a grin.

"Yes. No. I don't know." I'm so confused. "So I went to Parents' Night Out tonight at the new gymnastics place," I begin to tell her, "and it was awesome and I love doing gymnastics and being around gymnastics and my new friends that like it are so cool. And, well, I want to make this Level 3 team and mom says no."

"Did mom say no, or were you just being demanding at the wrong time?" I am silent, since the turd may be onto something and I hate it when she is right.

"I don't know," I sulk. I tuck my feet under the covers and look down at my black pajama shorts and pretend to study the red ladybugs on them.

"Why don't you just back off a little, work really hard in the class that mom is taking you to and see what happens?"

"Because I can't stand to wait," I whine. This has always been my problem.

"Hey, at least you have friends in this weird place. I haven't met anyone my age," she confessed with a tiny hint of jealousy, which I enjoyed for a brief moment. But then I felt bad for her, I guess I *have* met friends and she hasn't.

"Madi, maybe you could, you know, take time away from your old friends you're texting to make new ones?" I suggest. "There were lots of kids your age at the thing I went to tonight," I say.

"Maybe," she says as she walks out of the room. "Night, drama queen," she says closing the door.

"Night, turd," I reply.

Chapter 10

Handspring to Flat Back for Vault

"Good Morning, sunshine," my mom says as she pulls back the window shades revealing a bright, sunny morning.

"Ugh," I say, and roll over.

"Trista, it's past nine. Time to wake up. We have Saturday morning chores to do and we need to talk about what happened last night."

I've Got This!

Last night, last night, what happened last night?
Oh yeah, my mom was being unfair! But now it all
seems sort of silly. Maybe I did over react a little.

"Mom?" I ask, sitting up. "Why won't you let me do
team?" I try to ask as calmly as possible.

"I never said I wouldn't let you, I just reminded
you that we've never talked about it. You have to slow
down sometimes, make a plan, and discuss things with
your family." She walks over to my bed, sits on the edge
and pushes hair out of my face and tucks the strands
behind my ear. I love it when she does that. "So, how
about you take some time to get dressed and I will
meet you at breakfast and we can talk?"

"Okay," I agree and flop back down in my pillow.
She smiles gets up and silently walks out of my room. I
look up at my ceiling and think about the night before.
I learned vault in one night. Maybe the other events will
come just as easy. Then again, vault in Level 3 does not
actually use the vaulting table so it's more like tumbling.
Beam and bars are more different for me and I'm not
so sure.

I finally drag myself out of bed, get dressed in jean shorts and a red ribbed tank top, pull my hair back in a ponytail, and make my way to the breakfast table. My mom is slicing up fruit at the kitchen counter, my sister and dad are nowhere to be seen.

"Where is everyone?" I ask.

"Your sister is not down yet; I just woke her up too. Your dad is already working outside in the yard before it gets too hot."

"Oh," I say, and start eating the oatmeal and fruit she has put in front of me.

"Trista, do you want to explain to me what you have in mind for gymnastics?"

"Well," I stall, swirling around my oatmeal, feeling a little embarrassed now. "I really like it," I start, "but I don't like how young the kids are in my class. I want to be with kids my age. And competing sounds like fun. I want to do it as soon as I can," I explain.

"You want to be with kids your age or you want to be with Savannah?" she asks.

"Both," I answer quickly.

"You know, Savannah is seven and you like being with her."

"Yeah, but she doesn't seem that young, and the girls I met last night, Marissa and Alexis, are eight."

"Mm-hm," my mom muses. "I don't think that you can rush it, Trista. You learn as fast as you learn."

"Can I do an extra class? Is there another Level 2 class? Maybe I can go twice a week?" I blurt out, in desperation.

My mom just gives me a half smile and starts cleaning up her cutting board in the sink.

"Let's just stick with once a week and see how it goes. You may lose interest once summer gets going and you find other things to do."

It's annoying to me that my mom doesn't understand that I am never ever going to lose interest in this. Why would she think that? Okay, so maybe I didn't stick with piano, tennis, or soccer. But this is different. Gymnastics is so much more fun.

"Well, how can I learn faster?" I pout.

"Just work hard when you are there." My mom sets aside the cutting board and runs the knife under the water.

"That's it!" I say, "I need to be there. James said that if I keep going to Open Gym and PNO he will teach me stuff so I can catch up. He taught me vault last night. I know the Level 3 vault!" I say proudly.

"Who's James?" my mom asks, setting the knife on a towel to dry.

"A coach. The Level 3 coach. He taught me some tricks last night. Not tricks," I correct myself, "skills."

"You learned skills at Parents' Night Out?" she asks, looking up with interest.

I nod. "Can I go every week?" I have to almost bite my tongue to keep from whining and making her say no.

"I don't see why not, at least when we aren't busy."

I smile a huge smile. "Thanks! You're the best Mom ever!"

She smiles, "Of course I am. And if you are working hard in your class and hard at Parents' Night Out I will talk to Katie about when kids can change levels and learn more about how competitive gymnastics works, okay?"

I nod, eat a few bites, and add, "Can I go tell Savannah?"

"Chores first, then you can go over there and play on the grass the rest of the day."

Chapter 11

Backward Roll to Push-Up Position on Floor

I skip over to Savannah's house as soon as my chores are done. I hate Saturday chores, but at least they are done and I can play now. I walk up the few steps to her house and ring the doorbell. Savannah's mom answers the door and smiles when she sees me.

"Hi, Trista," she says.

"Can Savannah play?" I quickly ask.

"She's at gymnastics, but you guys can play when she gets back."

"Oh." I say deflated. "Every Saturday?" I ask, feeling cheated that I'm not good enough to go to gymnastics more than once a week.

"Just this summer so they can learn their routines for the fall," she smiles proudly. "Would after lunch work? I can have her go over to you?"

"Yeah, okay, that works," I reply.

She laughs, "Don't look so sad, she'll be home before you know it." She chuckles and waves to me as I make my way back to my boring chore-doing house.

I go to my room and try to find a good book to read while I wait for Savannah. It takes me a while, but I finally find a good one about a wacky school. I decide to take the book outside to wait for Savannah. Once I'm outside, I survey my new front yard. I haven't really spent a lot of time out here yet. There is a great tree with a trunk shaped like a Y, perfect for sitting with a book. I climb up easily and settle in with my book.

"Hey drama queen! How long have you been up there?" my sister asks, interrupting me from another time and place.

"I don't know," I answer, a little disoriented.

"Well, mom was looking for you for lunch, I'll let her know you are alive and just a weird monkey," she says and walks back into the house. A weird monkey? I smile. Monkeys swing. I don't mind being compared to a monkey. In fact, they do one-armed giants. I giggle to myself. I read a few more pages and then Mom comes out.

"Hey there sunshine, we thought we would join you out here. It's so nice out today; you have the right idea." She spreads out a blanket and sets down a plate of sandwiches, a container of veggies, and a bag of chips. Looking at the picnic spread out below me, I realize I am starving. I climb down from my perch and we eat for a while in silence. It is a perfect 80 degrees out with a little breeze ruffling my hair. I can look up in any direction and see giant charcoal jagged mountain peaks. One mountain even has snow on top and the contrast looks so beautiful against the gray rock and blue sky.

"The weather is like San Jose," I comment to my mom.

"Only in June, dork," my sister replies.

"Well, I know it will snow here, but why wouldn't it be like this all summer?" I ask my mom. In San Jose it was like this every day of the year except for one 'heat wave' that lasted about a week in the summer and one 'storm,' which was a few days of rain in the winter.

"I'm afraid all the seasons are more severe here than at home. According to the locals I have talked to it is only going to be this nice in June, then July and August get really hot," my mom answers.

"What happens in September?" my sister asks, and I'm glad she is not being a know-it-all for two seconds.

"It should cool down in September and be nice like today," my mom says, looking up at the mountains.

"And October?" I ask.

"I was told snow. The neighbors told me it can snow as early as October." I peer at my mom. She looks a little sad. This move must be hard on her too. She loved the nice days in San Jose and always had us eating outside. And she had loads of friends at her old job. Here she has decided to stay home with us and I wonder if she is missing all of those things.

"Do you like it here?" I ask my mom.

She looks at me, surprised. "I – I don't know yet. I'm enjoying the chance to be with you girls more and part of me is excited to experience four seasons."

"Do you miss work?" I ask.

She smiles, "Yes and no. I miss my colleagues and the challenges of the projects, but I'm having fun settling into the house and having time like this to stop and talk to you two." I keep eating and think about this for a minute. I guess we all have to adjust to the change.

As we are eating Savannah's mom's car pulls into her driveway. As soon as the car stops Savannah jumps out and runs over to us.

"I learned the floor routine today!" she announces, excitedly.

"You did?" I say in awe.

"Yeah, want to see?"

"Yes!" I answer honestly. She is already doing poses and leaps on the grass.

"How does it work?" my sister asks, "Your coach makes it up for you?"

"No," Savannah answers. "All Level 3s in the United States do this same routine. You don't get to do your own thing until Level 6."

"Well, that's boring," my too-honest and totally incorrect sister says.

"It can be a little boring for the parents," Savannah's mom says, walking up. "But good learning for kids this young. Really, at this age, anything they do is cute."

I look at Savannah with her blonde ponytail, big blue eyes, and baby cheeks, and I see her mom is right. Anything this girl does would be cute. I find myself wishing for the first time in my life that I was younger.

"What does the 'U' stand for?" my sister asks, referring to the little red U on the chest of Savannah's black leotard.

"Utah," her mom answers. "The University of Utah has a phenomenal gymnastics team and that is a mini-version of their warm up leo."

My mom and Savannah's mom start talking about the college program and I get up and join Savannah. Pretty soon she is teaching me the routine she learned this morning. She teaches me this funny backwards roll into a push up position.

"Why is this in the routine? It's such a weird skill," I ask, making sure to say 'skill' instead of 'trick.'

"James said it's a drill for back extension rolls," she explains

"What's a back extension roll?" I ask

"You roll backwards and then pop up into a handstand, like this." She tries one and fails miserably, but I get what she is trying to do. I try some and it's harder than it seems it should be. After several times of rolling back and flopping over on the grass we get the

giggles and can't seem to stop laughing.

"You girls! I'm not sure what you were trying to do,

but that was entertaining," her mom says warmly. Then

she turns to my mom. "Am I okay to leave Savannah

here to play for a bit?" she asks.

"Of course, I plan to be here all day anyway."

Savannah and I are delighted to hear we get to

keep playing and we go back to having her teach

me the Level 3 floor routine. Once I have the routine

memorized we start pretending we are in a meet and

judging each other. Doing an entire routine is way more

fun than just the round-off back handspring we were

doing the other day. And then it hits me, I am doing the

Level 3 floor routine! I can officially do floor and vault.

All I need to learn is bars and beam; I've got this!

Chapter 12

Mil Circle on Bars

I stare down at the blister that just ripped open on my hand. I'm at my Level 2 class and we are working mil circles. Mil circles that I can never quite get. "Melony," I say to my coach, "I got a rip."

"Good job!" she smiles. "That means you're working hard."

Sometimes the coaches around here are so weird. Why would she be happy about my painful rip?

"Go to the office and ask a coach in there for a rip kit and come back to me."

"You mean Samantha, at the reception desk?" I ask.

"No, don't bother Sam, she is way too busy at this hour. Go behind her desk to the coaches' office; someone will be in there and can get you what you need."

I make my way around a bunch of kids and parents in the lobby, go behind Samantha's desk, to the coaches' office, and timidly walk in. I haven't been in here before. I scan the room; there are eight desks, but only one person is in the room. She looks up at me as I walk in.

"What can I do for you, hon?" she asks.

"I need a rip kit," I say. She smiles and stands up and walks to a credenza on the far right wall. Sitting on top of it are a pair of small nail scissors sitting in a jar of blue water. She hands me the scissors, a tube of cream, and white athletic tape. She tells me to bring back everything when I am done and I assure her I will.

"You can go back out this way," she says pointing to a door that connects directly to the training area. "The lobby is crazy this time of day."

As I make my way back to my coach I pass the beam area where James and the Level 3's are working. I smile at Savannah and she waves at me. She is doing handstands on high beam and I am so jealous. James sees her waving and looks over at me.

"What have you got there?" he asks me.

"A rip kit," I answer. "I got my first rip."

"Let me see," he says.

"Oh no, don't show him!" Marissa warns.

I walk over to where James is standing and I extend my hand out for him to see. I am happy to get attention for my pain.

"Congratulations!" he says and slaps my hand. Hard.

"Ouch! Why would you do that?" I yelp, as I pull back my stinging hand.

"That's what all gymnasts get with their first rip, it's a right of passage," He says happily. "You are officially a bar worker!" I must still look stunned and confused because he adds, "Bar workers are tough, so you can handle a little high five after a rip."

I'm not sure what to think of this. *Is he teasing me, or is this really a tradition?* I look up questioningly at the girls watching me from the high beams.

"He slapped mine way harder," Marissa boasts.

"Mine was bleeding," Alexis adds.

"Both of you are exaggerating, your rip-high-fives were just like hers," Paige says.

This makes me feel a little better, but there is still a throbbing heartbeat inside my hand.

"Keep up the hard work, Trista. Now get back to your class," James instructs.

I leave the beam area and hustle back to Melony over at the quad bars and hand her the rip kit. She asks for my hand and I hesitate.

"I won't slap it like James does, that's totally a guy thing." I still don't move my hand toward her. She yells over to James, "James, at least wait until they are Level 3 before you initiate them!"

"It was her first rip!" he yells back, "We were never going to have that moment again!"

Melony turns back to me. "Trista, I promise I won't 'high five' you. I just need to cut away the dead skin."

I finally give her my hand and she does just that. She carefully cuts away the dead skin, which surprisingly, doesn't hurt. Then she put some cream on it and added the athletic tape to my hand in an unusual way; winding the tape between my fingers and down my hand, around my wrist, and back up to my fingers. She did all this while giving corrections to the rest of the girls on bars.

"Why not just tape it straight across my hand?" I ask when she rips the tape from the roll and finishes up.

"Because it will just roll up on your hand when you swing on the bars."

"Swing on the bars? But aren't I done?" I ask.

"Why would you be done? We have 15 more minutes on bars, go return the rip kit and come back for back hip circles."

I've Got This!

What? I'm done because my hand hurts! This sport is crazy. I didn't know about pain and hard work when I watched it on TV. In fact, I've never thought about pain and hard work when I watch Kayla and the other competitive girls in the gym. I wonder how many rips they've had. And did it hurt this bad? And did they get a rip-high-five? And did they keep swinging on the bars? I know the answer to all of these questions is yes. I look around at all the girls in shimmery leotards, looking so feminine and graceful, and I realize something. They are all tough as nails.

Chapter 13

Cartwheel to Handstand, Twist Dismount on Beam

"When'd you learn that?" James asks, referring to the Level 3 beam routine I am practicing on the low beam. I'm at another Parents' Night Out, desperately trying to improve on bars and beam so I can move up to Level 3. There are only three weeks left of summer. My mom did talk to the gym owner, Katie, about team and how I move up to Level 3. Katie said she or James would test me at the end of the summer and see if I'm ready.

"Savannah taught me in my front yard," I answer James.

He chuckles. "Well it's nice having you two as neighbors," he says. "Do you know the floor routine too, or just beam?"

"Floor, too," I answer as I keep walking through the Level 3 beam routine on the low beam.

"Why are you on low beam?" he asks.

"Hey coach," a boy says as he walks by James and high fives him.

"What's up Drew, kips tonight?" James asks him. The boy continues to walk toward the high bar as he passes James, but now he is walking backwards to keep the conversation going.

"Yeah, and can you spot me on back tucks, too?" the boy asks. As I look at this boy, my stomach does a little flutter; he's really cute. He has blond hair that is sticking up in spikes every which way and the greenest eyes I have ever seen. He has on athletic shorts and a gray zippered hoodie. Seriously, who has eyes that green besides a cartoon character?

"Sure, kips first, warm up and let me know when you're ready. Where's Alexis?" James asks.

"Saying bye to our mom, I guess." The boy shrugs. With that statement I put together that this is Alexis' brother. I didn't know she had a brother who did gymnastics. James nods and turns back to me. "Why are you on the low beam?" he asks again.

I am a little disoriented from watching the boy, so all I can manage to say to James is a moronic, "I dunno."

James chuckles, knowingly. "Trista, you are a great floor worker. All beam is, is floor in a straight line."

"A straight line four inches wide and four feet off the ground."

"Do you know how to fall?" he asks.

"What?" I stop my dance moves and look at him.

"Do you know how to fall?" he repeats.

"Is there a secret to it?" I ask, confused.

I've Got This!

"Yes, aim for your feet and keep your arms in front of you. Maybe if you know how to fall out of your skills, you won't be as scared of high beam."

This makes sense in a weird way, so I ask, "How do I learn to fall?"

He smiles and gives me a little shove. "Hey!" I yell as I plop back on the soft mats and land on my bottom.

"See how your arms are behind you?" he asks. I look down and see I tried to catch myself with my arms behind me. I nod.

"That's your instinct, but a bad one. If you are taking a big fall and put your arms back to catch yourself, you may break your arm." *Break my arm?* I think he is making my fear of beam worse. "Stand up, let's try again."

I stand up and step on to the low beam. "Now, keep your arms in front of you and round your back," he says as he shoves me again. I do what he says and I feel myself land on my bottom and roll onto my back so my hands don't catch me, but it's not scary.

"Good!" he smiles. "Do you ever watch basketball on TV?" he asks.

"No, but my dad does sometimes," I answer.

"Next time he's watching basketball, watch how they fall. Their arms are always in front and they round their back and slide on their bum and lower back, a much safer way to fall." This is such new and odd information - learning to fall? Who would have thought it was a skill?

"Also, on beam, you can usually tell a fall is coming and have time to get to your feet. You just need to learn how to do that." I am listening very carefully; this is fascinating.

"For example," he continues, "out of the handstand you need to be able to twist off and land on your feet when you go too far over the back side. It's the Level 3 dismount so you have to learn to do it anyway.

"In fact, let's do some now," he instructs.

I've Got This!

He spots me on handstand twisting off on the low beam until I have it. Then he leaves to go help Drew with kips on the men's high bar.

After I have done a few handstands on my own, Alexis walks in with three bigger boys. One rubs her head with his knuckles and then runs off to the pit. "Hey!" she yells and adjusts her headband and frowns at me. "He is such a pain."

"You have another brother?" I guess.

"Another? I have four stupid brothers."

"All of them are your brothers?" I asked shocked. I look over to the three boys who are running and jumping over mats and doing sloppy twists in the air as they jump. I see the resemblance; they are all blond and fair like Alexis.

"There are five of you?" I ask, shock clear in my voice.

"Sure," she says, stepping up on the low beam with me. "We're Mormon, and we tend to have big families." I remember a Mormon family in San Jose and I guess they did have a lot of kids.

"Yeah, but five? Wow."

"My mom has seven siblings and my dad has nine," she says not really bothered by my gaping mouth.

"So, are you going to have seven siblings too?" I ask.

"No. My mom really wanted a girl and now that I'm here, she says she's done. Plus, she says five is the new seven."

"Are all your brothers in gymnastics?" I ask as I see Drew climbing up on to a block so he can reach the boys' high bar. James is standing on the block with him, ready to help him with kips.

"No, just Drew. The others are into baseball and basketball, but they like to come to PNO to just mess around."

"How old is Drew?" I ask casually. I secretly want to know everything about him.

"He's nine, just one year older than us. He's in fourth grade," she answers. "So, what are you working over here?"

I can tell she is done talking about her family so I answer, "James says I need to learn how to fall."

"Well, you're not getting much practice from the low beam," she laughs. This makes me giggle and I know she's right.

"I'm not ready to do handstands on high beam," I explain

"Well, let's fall doing other stuff," she says stepping off of the low beam and walking past the medium beam and climbing up on to a high beam. "Let's do a split jump and see who has the best fall," she challenges.

I take the challenge and climb up on the high beam next to her. We both do a split jump, land back on our feet, and then dramatically jump off the beam to the mats below. I notice she keeps her arms in front and I try to remember to do that, too. It's so silly, it's funny. We do this with everything; half turns, leaps, poses, all of it. By the time James comes back from helping Drew we have some serious giggles. In fact, we are laughing so hard Alexis has started hiccupping.

"How's it going over here?" he asks.

"We are practicing [hiccup] falling!" Alexis says.

"Great," he says smiling, "I want to see."

I stop laughing long enough to climb up on the beam and do a sloppy leap, land on my feet, and jump off the side. I roll around laughing at this ridiculous new skill.

"That was the ugliest leap I have ever seen," he says with a grin.

This stops my laughing and I say, "Then why are you happy?" I ask.

"Because in the time I left to go help Drew with kips, you learned to be friends with beam. You aren't scared anymore." He grins. *Wait, what? Is that true?* I open my mouth to ask how he knows this and he's gone. He is walking over to spot some girls who are tumbling into the pit.

I look over at Alexis, whose giggles have died down and now she is just hiccupping. She grins as me, "I didn't know you were afraid of beam."

"I wasn't," I lied, "just of the handstand."

Chapter 14

Bridge Kick Over on Floor

"You are so close," Carmen says as I swing backwards out of my mil circle. I can't quite seem to get it around. This is my last bar workout before the end of the summer. Katie has agreed to test me this Friday at Open Gym for Level 3. It turns out my Level 2 class has not been so bad. Melony is a really nice coach and I enjoy working out with Carmen. We always share the same bar and beam when we can.

I've Got This!

"I have got to get this before Friday," I tell her.

"What's Friday?" Carmen asks.

"Katie is testing me for Level 3," I explain. Carmen looks surprised at this.

"Wow," she says, "you've learned fast this summer."

"So have you," I say, now feeling bad that I might move on without her. "Maybe you should be tested too?"

"No, I don't have very many of my Level 3 skills. I can't do the mil circle or single leg shoot through on bars. And I can't do a bridge kick over, or a round-off back handspring on floor." *I don't have my mil circle or single leg shoot through either; does that mean I'm not ready?* This thought makes me jump up and try the mil circle again. I put my hands in the front grip, lift my leg up and swing around. Just as I am about to come around to the top of the bar I lose speed and fall back the other way. Dang it, this is hard.

"Do one more skill, girls, and we are going to floor." Melony calls out. No, no, no, I didn't get it yet. And I don't need to go to floor, I need to stay on bars!

Carmen sees my face and says, "Maybe it will just click on Friday. You never know." This is a nice thought but I don't think so. I do one last terrible mil circle and rotate to floor. Usually I love floor, but I just can't get excited about it right now. Melony has been really cool with me on floor this summer. She has taught me front handsprings and spots me on back tucks when I finish the Level 2 floor workout. Today I go through the motions of floor and don't ask to do anything extra. I can't believe summer is almost over and I couldn't pull it together to make Level 3.

When the workout is over, I mope over to my mom's car. She immediately sees my pathetic mood. "What's wrong, Sunshine?" she asks.

"I don't think the testing on Friday is going to go very well."

"Why wouldn't it? You have worked so hard this summer and learned so much," she points out.

97

"Yeah, but I don't have all my Level 3 skills. I still can't do much on bars."

"What about the pull up? Didn't you get that a couple of weeks ago? You were so excited. Isn't that a Level 3 skill?" she asks.

"Pullover," I correct her, "yeah, but there are three other things on bars I can't do."

"What are they?" she asks.

"A front hip circle, single leg shoot through, and front mil circle," I answer. I know she has no idea what I am talking about.

"Well, Trista, just do your best on Friday with Katie and let her decide what level you should be. Don't give up before you have even tried."

Don't give up before I try. I hold onto this thought, but all I keep imagining is me falling on all my bars skills while Katie is watching. And I have gone and made such a big deal all summer about being a Level 3 this fall that I will just die of embarrassment if I don't make it.

At dinner I push around my food and give only one word answers. "What happened to you, drama queen? I'm actually missing all your theatrics," Madison

jabs. I roll my eyes at her.

"Nothing," I mumble.

"And you guys think I'm moody,"

Madison continues.

"Let it go Madison," my mom says, "She's just

nervous for Friday." *Nervous?* I don't think that's it. More

like terrified. I don't really get nervous when I show off.

But I am just not ready.

That night I lay in bed going through the Level

3 bar routine over and over in my head. Then I hear

Carmen's words. *Maybe it will just click on Friday.* I sure

hope so, I think, as I finally drift off to sleep.

Chapter 15

Front Handspring on Floor

"I'll be up in the parent viewing area, okay?" My mom heads upstairs. It's my testing day. We set this up because I was determined to be a Level 3 by the end of the summer. It's still what I want, I'm just not sure I can make it. Savannah, Marissa, and Alexis are going to be here later for PNO and I am nervous about what I am going to tell them if I don't make it. I give my mom a weak smile and make my way into the workout area. I head over to the end of the red strip that is by floor to warm up.

"Hey, Trista," Katie opens one of the glass doors and pokes her head in. I look up at her, "Warm up on floor first because floor will fill up fast when more kids get here for Open Gym. I have a couple more things to do in the office and then I'll be with you, okay?" I swallow hard and nod my head.

After a few minutes I stand up and start warming up all the floor skills that I know are required for Level 3. I warm up the bridge kick over, handstand forward roll, back roll to push up position, and round-off back handspring. I even think to do a leap or two.

"Impressive, even doing your leaps," Katie comments as she walks up to me with a clipboard in her hand. "You ready?" I nod nervously. "Okay, since you are doing leaps, start there. Let's see your leap on each side." I show her my leaps, which are fine, I guess.

Then she has me do all the skills in the Level 3 routine, plus a few extra. "Melony says she taught you front handsprings; do you want to show me?" I smile and happily show her my new front handsprings. She writes notes down and says, "Your floor is really nice, as you know. Let's set up vault before the floor gets too busy."

The 8-inch mats are stacked neatly at the very end of the red tumbling strip. All we have to do is take two of them down so there is only a stack of four and add the spring board to the end. "I'll go get the spring board, you pull off two of these," Katie says referring to the stack of 8-inchers. I do as she says and when she comes back and sets the spring board down she says, "Go for it, let's see what you've got."

I run, hurdle onto the spring board, jump to a handstand, and fall with a flat back onto the mats. Vault is a really fun sensation, especially the falling part. "Good," says Katie. "A couple more with a little better form and we can be done." Oh yeah, my form. Sometimes I get so caught up in the feeling of gymnastics and how to do the skill, I forget to squeeze my legs together and keep them straight. I run and do another vault and I remember to squeeze my legs. "Much better, I knew you could do a pretty one. Once more like that and then to beam." I do one more just like that and this time I really enjoy the feeling of doing a skill well. When I am done I wave up to my mom in the viewing area and she waves back. Then Katie and I head over to the beam area.

Beam is not as easy as floor and vault, but I am not afraid of it anymore either. I am on high beam and Katie asks me do leaps, straight jumps, half turns, and a cross handstand. I can do all of these skills, but Melony says they are 'small.' I wonder if Katie thinks the same thing. And what does that mean anyway? I wish I would have asked Melony when I had the chance. "Can you do the dismount?" Katie asks.

"I can do it on low beam, I need a spot on high beam," I answer honestly.

"Okay, let me see a few on low beam and I'll spot you on high beam."

I jump down and go over to the low beam and do three of them and then Katie says, "Those are fine, jump up here and I will help you." I climb up onto the high beam and I hesitate. Only James and Melony have spotted me on these; does Katie know what she is doing? Then I remember that she spots the high level girls on all sorts of things, and I also remember this is my chance to become a Level 3. So I kick up into a handstand, Katie holds my hips and centers me, and I twist off and fall to the ground in the dismount. "Very good. You're really close to doing that on your own. Do a couple more." I climb up and do another one and I notice that she barely touches me when I am in handstand before I twist off for the landing. It was a little scary, but super awesome that I almost did it by myself. "One more," she says. I climb up again, but now I am scared that she will spot me too lightly again, or not at all.

"You are going to spot me, right?" I confirm

"Only if you need it," she responds. This makes my stomach sink a little.

"I need it!" I begin to panic. She smiles and says, "Trista, I have been doing this a long time, I know a good handstand on beam when I see one. You need to trust me and you need to trust yourself." With that she lifts her arm ready for my handstand.

I take a deep breath and kick up to handstand. She barely touches me as I go all the way into handstand before I twist off. That was so close; I almost did it all by myself! I want to try again but Katie says, "Good. Let's go to bars."

That immediately ruins my elation. I am dreading bars.

Chapter 16

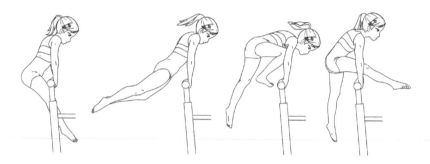

Single Leg Shoot Though on Bars

I start nibbling on the hang nail on my pinky finger as we walk over to bars. It is not going to go as well as the other three events. Carmen's words come back to me. *Maybe it will just click on Friday.* This is really my only hope, so I hang on to the thought.

"Start with your pull over," Katie instructs. This, at least, I can do. I step up to the bar and kick my legs up for my pull over, but they flop back down. *What just happened? I can do a pullover.* I try again, and they flop back down again. "Keep your chin on your chest, Trista, you're throwing your head back." Oh yeah, Melony says to look at the bar. I pause and stand with my feet on the ground, hands on the bar and think about what I am doing. I look at the bar, kick my feet up, get my hips on the bar, and rotate until I am up on the bar in a support position. I did it! I knew I could do my pullover. "Good, again," Katie says. I jump down and do it again, remembering to think about what I'm doing. "Okay, back hip circle," she says. This one I can do, too, and I do a few with ease for her. "Single leg shoot through," she says. Oh no. I can't do this one.

"Can you spot me?" I ask weakly.

"Try a few and let's see how close you get." Oh brother, I can tell her right now I am not going to get very close. I cast up as high as I can (which is not very high), tuck my knee up to my chest and try kicking one leg between my arms. And I slam my foot into the bar instead. "You are going to have to cast higher and get

your shoulders in front more if you want to make that,"
Katie says. "Try again." And I do. I try three more times,
once I slammed both feet into the bar and the other
two times I got the one foot into the bar, but not over
it and through my arms. "Okay, let me spot one." She
spots me and with her help I make it easily. I wish it felt
like that without her help.

"All right, let's see your mil circle," she says. The
same thing happens with the front mil circle. I fail
miserably on three or four. She spots me and I can do
it. Repeat that for the front hip circle. By the time bars
is over I feel completely deflated. I can only do two of
the skills required on bars in Level 3. I think I just blew it.

"Okay, Trista, great job today. Thank you for
coming in and working so hard."

"Welcome," I mumble. *What now?* I have to know,
but I am too flustered to ask. Luckily she starts to tell me.

"You are an unusual case, Trista. You are ready
on three events, but not bars," she says, pointing out
the obvious.

"I know," I say. "So I have to stay Level 2 until my bars gets better?" I ask. When the words are out of my mouth, I feel my throat go dry. I am so mad at myself, how did I let this happen?

"I'm not sure. I'm going to have to talk to James about it and get back to you. He is the compulsories coach, so it's mostly his decision."

"Okay," I squeak out of my chalky mouth.

"Let's go talk to your mom," Katie says and we start walking to the glass doors that lead out to the lobby.

My mom has come down from the viewing area and meets us in the lobby. "How'd it go?" she asks, although I'm not sure how she could have missed how it went. She saw the disaster on bars.

"She is amazing on floor, as you know," Katie begins. "And her vault is a typical Level 3 vault. Beam is coming along, although she is still timid. Bars is the real problem." Katie admits.

"I saw that," my mom says honestly. "So what do you recommend?"

"Well, we have a couple of options. She can continue with Level 2 until she is ready on bars," when I hear this I feel tears stinging hot in the back of my eyes. "Or she can work out with the Level 3 non-competitive group."

Neither of these options appeal to me and I sneak away to go put my flip flops and t-shirt on before I cry in front of Katie. I go over to the cubbies and get my shoes while my mom keeps talking to Katie. I am supposed to stay for the rest of Open Gym and PNO, but I just don't want to tonight. I blink back my tears and take a deep breath. What am I going to do now? I go back into the training area and over to the drinking fountain and get a drink of water, then I head back into the lobby to where my mom and Katie are finishing up their conversation.

"Thank you for taking the time to evaluate her tonight. Call me after you speak with James."

"Will do," Katie says as she walks behind the reception desk. "Good job today and all summer, Trista. You will be fine. It just may take longer than you expect," she says to me. I know she is trying to be nice, but at the moment I hate what she just said.

My mom looks down at me and sees I have my shoes and t-shirt on and am standing by the door. "I thought you were staying," she says.

I shake my head, "I don't feel like it tonight."

My mom walks over to me and puts her arm around my shoulder and takes me through the front doors. "Okay, Sunshine," she says, giving me a nice mommy squeeze. And this is what finally makes me cry.

Chapter 17

Back Hip Circle on Bars

"Wake up, Sunshine," my mom says coming into my room. "Time for Saturday morning chores!"

"Ugh," I say and roll over.

"Oh no, you don't. Look at this room, you need to get it all clean and tidy. Let's start off on the right foot for school this week."

"Don't remind me, school starts this week," I moan.

"Why don't you want to start school?
You've made so many friends already," she says,
genuinely confused.

"Because none of my gym friends go to Hilltop,
except Savannah, and she is starting second grade
and I am starting third grade, so we won't even see
each other." I explain.

"Well, you made friends so easily this summer;
I'm sure it will be the same at school. Now get up,
lazy bones." She walks out with purpose, to go wake
my sister.

I get up, eat breakfast, and take my sweet time
cleaning my room. I figure if it takes me forever to clean
my room I won't have to do other chores. Then I get
distracted by a book and find myself laying on my bed
reading when the doorbell rings.

I hear my sister get it, and then she yells up the
stairs, "Trista, it's for you!"

I roll off my bed and come out of my room. I can
see from the top of the stairs that it's Savannah. I skip
down the stairs to see her.

"Hey!" I say.

"Hey," she says. "Want to play at my house?" I can tell she has just come from Saturday practice because she is still wearing a leotard and little shorts. This time it's a red, silver, and blue leo with silver shorts over it. She looks like a mini-Olympian. I look over my shoulder at my mom.

"It's fine," my mom says. I know my room is not clean yet, and normally she wouldn't let me go if it's not clean. She must feel really bad for me and my flub last night.

I grab my flip-flops by the door, before my mom can change her mind, I walk outside into the hot August day. As Savannah and I walk back to her house she asks me, "Where were you last night? You said you were going to be at Parents' Night Out."

"I know. I just didn't feel like it," I say. This stops her walking and she looks at me.

"Well, we were sad you weren't there. Paige came and I wanted you to get to know Paige better."

I'm quiet since I don't know what to say. We reach her house and she says, "Do you want to play gymnastics on the grass or go inside?"

I stand there for a minute, not sure what I want to do. We have never had an awkward moment like this before in our friendship.

"Play gymnastics, I guess," I say, kicking a pebble in her driveway with my toe.

"What happened?" Savannah asks.

"What do you mean?" I play dumb. Savannah is only seven, she may not know what's going on.

"I mean, how did your tryouts go? Is that why you're being weird?" she asks. So much for her not knowing what's going on.

"Savannah, it was terrible!" I confess as I sink down on the grass next to the driveway.

"How terrible?" she says, sitting down next to me.

"Well, floor was fine. And vault, you know." She nods and I continue, "Beam was okay, not great. But bars was a mess. I can't do any of it." I whine.

"You can do your pullover and back hip circle," she says.

"Yeah, but that's it." I lay back in the grass. "What am I going to do?"

She lays next to me and stacks her hands behind her head. "It's a bummer because I wanted you to be in class with me, but we still live next door. And you like that Carmen girl in your class, right?" She asks.

"Yeah, she's cool."

"And lots of us take a while to finish levels. My mom wanted me to compete last fall, but James said I should wait until this year."

"Really?" I turn my head to look at her.

"Yeah, I mean, you only have to be six years old to compete Level 3, so my mom wanted me to compete last year. But James said I wasn't ready."

I think about this for a moment. I can't imagine Savannah even smaller than she is now, competing. I wonder if there will be girls that young competing against her this fall.

"What do you think? Did you want to compete last year?" I ask.

"I wanted to. But the routines were more confusing for me last year than they are now. I couldn't do them unless James wrote an L and R on my hands and feet for left and right. I felt bad I disappointed my mom, but James was really nice about it and he talked to her for me."

I think about this for a minute as I lay in the grass and look up at the clouds. The air is hot and dry and when there's a breeze it feels like a blow dryer in my face. I think about Savannah and how I just assumed everything came easy for her. I guess it's not really easy for anyone, and somehow this makes me feel better.

Chapter 18

Underswing Dismount on Bars

Savannah and I ended up playing with her princess dolls inside because it was too hot out. The time passed so fast I was surprised when Savannah's mom told us it was time for me to go home for dinner. As I make my way home I think back over my day yesterday and heave a big sigh. At home I find my mom and my sister out back setting up an outdoor dinner.

"Hey," I say and my mom looks up.

"I was just going to send Madison over to get you. Did you have a fun afternoon?" she asks. I nod. "How are you feeling?"

"Better," I answer and I am surprised that that is how I honestly feel.

"What's the big deal?" my sister asks with all her sass. "It's not like someone died, you just couldn't do it is all. We all knew that might happen."

"Madi," my mom warns, but I cut her off.

"Hey!" I yell in protest, "Maybe I couldn't do it yesterday, but I *will* do it! You wait and see!"

"Whatever," she says and saunters into the house to get more supplies for dinner. She makes me so mad.

"Trista?" My mom says, getting my attention away from the turd-bucket.

"What?" I say with an annoyed tone, even though my mom is not the one I am annoyed at. She knows this and ignores it.

"James called," she says.

"He did?" I say, surprised. "Why?" I ask.

"To talk about your gymnastics," she answers.

"Well, was there much to talk about? I mean I can't do Level 3 bars."

"He and I talked for a long time about a lot of different options."

"Really? Like what?" I say, curious now.

She pulls out a patio chair and sits on it. "Well, you can stay in Level 2 until your bars are better," I nod and she continues, "or you can move to Level 3 and just not compete this year, or you can compete Level 3 except on bars."

"What?" I say getting excited, "I can do that?"

"James says you can. He says you have to still train bars, but for now you can scratch bars until you are ready to compete them. Scratching means you sit out during the bars rotation at meets. He said he was really impressed with how hard you worked this summer and thinks bars will come along in time. He said you are very ready on floor and vault and average on beam."

This is all true. But I can't believe he would make such a big exception for me. What an awesome coach. "He also said you still have to eventually catch up on bars because you cannot move up to Level 4 unless you can do all four events." I nod, taking in this bit of information.

Finally, everything is starting to sink in, "So, I can practice with Level 3?" I ask.

"If that's what you want," my mom answers.

"And you'll take me to practice two days a week?" I ask and she nods with a grin.

"And I can compete this fall?" I ask, my heart is starting to pound at this possibility.

"On everything except bars. If you want to," she answers.

"Mom! I want to! I want to! What'd you tell him?" I screech, jumping up and down.

"I told him I would talk to you," she says laughing.

"Call him back! Call him back now! Can I start Level 3 this week? Monday? When is the first meet? Oh my gosh, I have to go tell Savannah!"

My mom is laughing and pulls me in for a hug. "Good job, Sunshine," she says.

My sister shows up and says, "Drama queen is back. That's good, I kind of missed you." And she tugs on my hair playfully. I smile up at her in return.

"You knew didn't you?" I ask Madison.

"Yeah, I was just messing with you," she says. "I like to see you fired up."

"You are such a turd!" I smile back.

"Yep, and don't forget it." She says, and takes a seat next to mom.

I wiggle out of my mom's hug and I run in place, "Can I go tell Savannah?"

"Yes, but be back in ten, dinner is almost ready," she replies.

"I will," I yell over my shoulder as I run around the side of the house to the front where I sprint to Savannah's house.

This is going to be the best year ever! I am going to be a competitive gymnast with the coolest girls on the planet! And I can catch up on bars and win floor at every meet! I've got this!

Up Next?

Savannah's Story!

Book 2 in the Perfect Balance Gymnastics Series

Nothing Better Than Gym Friends

Chapter 1

The bell rings for morning recess and Megan and I sprint to the monkey bars on the playground as fast as we can. There are only three bars, if we get there first we don't have to wait.

"We're going to make it today, Savannah," Megan says running beside me. And she is right, we are the first second grade class to get out to recess and the playground is empty. We run and jump on a bar next to each other. I do a pull over to get up on the bar and Megan hooks a leg through to get herself up. Then she starts to swing around fast with one knee hooked around the bar and I start doing continuous back hip circles. We are having so much fun spinning and spinning.

"How do you do it without your knee hooked?" Megan asks. I stop and I'm about to explain when I am interrupted.

"Hey, Megan! Why don't you walk with us?" Megan turns her head and there is Lily standing with her arm hooked to Sarah's. I look at Megan, who seems startled.

Megan looks at me, shrugs, and says, "I think I'm going to walk with them for a bit, bye Savannah." And just like that she jumps down from the bar, and runs over to Lily and links arms with her. The three of them walk off with Sarah and Megan's heads tilted in toward Lily's to hear what she is saying.

I've stopped swinging as I watch them walk away. I don't feel like swinging anymore so I jump down. I walk over to the edge of the play area where there is curbing. I step up on the curbing, which is about the size of a balance beam, and I start walking on it and thinking. *Why wasn't I invited to walk with those girls?* If they knew me better I'm sure they would have invited me to walk with them. I'm nice and my friends at gymnastics all like me. I circle the playground area a few more times on the curbing before recess is over. Playing without Megan is so boring.

"Then when I got to the line to go inside Lily told me Megan is her second best friend and can't play on the bars with me anymore," I tell Trista. I'm next door at Trista's house playing before practice. I love hanging out with her. I wish it could be this easy and fun with the girls at my school. Well, Trista does go to Hilltop

Elementary too, but she is in third grade and I am in

second grade so we don't have recess together.

"Well that's stupid, Megan likes playing on the bars

with you," Trista replies.

"Not anymore."

"What does Megan say about not playing on the

bars anymore?" Trista asks me.

"Megan doesn't say anything, I don't

understand," I confess.

"Well, it's dumb, do what you want at recess and

don't worry about those girls," Trista says. I know Trista

means well, but how can I do what I want if there is no

one to play with? "Anyway, we have a fun weekend

coming up," Trista continues.

She's right, we have our first gymnastics meet

this weekend and after the meet our teammate,

Marissa, is having a birthday party. I'm excited for both

and I realize I don't need Lily and Megan to be my

friends, I'm going to have a great weekend with my

gymnastics friends.

"Are you nervous?" Trista asks me.

"Nervous about what?"

"The meet, silly!" she shrieks.

"Well, no. Don't we just do what we have been doing in practice?" I ask.

"Yeah, but people are going to be watching and taking pictures and there will be another team there, or maybe two, and we want to win!" she says, skipping around her room in a circle.

"Win?" I ask. "How do we win?" I should know this. I mean, my mom takes me to the University of Utah gymnastics meets and they always win but I'm not sure what that means. I know they each get scores and one person wins in the Olympics, but how does a team win?

"We add up all our scores or something, I'm not sure," Trista admits as she flops on her bed and rolls to her tummy. She leans over her bed and puts her hands on the ground. Her straight brown hair falls upside down as she bounces to a handstand. "All I know is," she huffs from her handstand, "that I want be the best and I want to earn a medal." Then she lets her handstand fall onto the bed and is on her stomach again.

A medal? I look at her laying on her belly. "How do you know about medals?" I ask.

"Kayla from the gym told me. She said that at most meets you get ribbons or little medals and that at some you get really big medals or even little trophies." Trista bounces up to a handstand for a second and drops to her belly in a hollow body position and bounces back up to handstand. Even though she is holding a handstand she keeps talking. "She said big medals and trophies are more common in the higher levels like 7 and 8." Trista is getting a little out of breath now as she drops her handstand back to her tummy on her bed and stays there.

"Girls! Five minutes!" Trista's mom yells up at us. Trista hops up and runs over to her dresser drawers. At the same time, I pick up the duffel bag of leotards that I brought with me.

"What leotard do you want to wear?" I ask, as I dump the contents of the duffel bag on the floor.

"I don't need one today, my mom bought me a new one for making Level 3." Trista worked so hard over the summer to become a Level 3, and I am so glad she did because now I have a friend and neighbor on my same team.

She pulls out her new leotard and holds it up for me. The bodice is a beautiful black shimmer with zebra print on the tank shoulders and top half of the back with lime green piping on the edges.

"Oh, Trista, that one is so fun and so you," I smile.

"I know, my mom almost didn't get it because it was so expensive, but I think she finally felt bad I was always wearing your leos," she says as she steps out of her jeans and into her new leotard. "Can I still borrow some shorts though?" she asks standing in her new leotard.

I frown at my huge pile of leotards and matching shorts and wonder how much it cost my mom. She just buys them for me all the time. I don't have to work for them like Trista did.

"Yeah, sure," I say and bend down and grab a pair of black shorts from the pile and toss them to her.

I guess I can't worry about Megan right now, it's time for practice.

For more information about the Perfect Balance Gymnastics Series visit melisatorres.com or facebook.com/pbgseries

About the Author

Melisa grew up in San Jose, California where she trained at Almaden Valley Gymnastics Club for ten years. She then went to compete for Utah State University where she was a two-time Academic All-American and team captain. Gymnastics taught Melisa how to be fit for life. She stays fit by weight lifting and dancing.

Melisa is a single mother to two active boys. Their favorite things to do together are skiing, swimming, going to the library, and dancing in the kitchen.